Addie's One Wish
to The Brightest Star

By

Gloria St. Joy
Illustrated by Dori Gonzalez

This story is dedicated to my brother and sister, Danny and Doris, with love.

Table of Contents

My Favorite Rag Doll Sophie

1

My Grandma's Paper Dolls

Eight-year-old Addie Zanini longed to be a big sister. She'd wanted a little brother or sister for as long as she could remember. Her friends, Mary Ellen and Tiana, had younger brothers and sisters and she wanted them too. To her, family meant having a little brother or sister.

One Friday evening, just before bedtime, Addie hurried to her room and played with her rag doll, Sophie. She thought she and Sophie looked a lot alike. They both had dark hair, short bangs, and wore their hair in two ponytails, but Addie's eyes were brown and Sophie's eyes were blue.

After Addie had played with Sophie for a while, she cradled her in her arms and looked out her bedroom window. "Sophie," she said, "it's time to make our wish. Let's close our eyes real tight. No peeking! Don't let any light in. Now let's make our wish." *Swoosh!* Addie held onto Sophie and stood still as she pictured her wish floating away to hook up with the brightest star. She called it the lucky star.

Once Addie had made her wish, her

mother came into her bedroom. "Addie, how would you like to go shopping with me tomorrow? I want to buy a blouse for your grandmother for her birthday."

"Sure! I like to go shopping. Is Grandma coming with us?"

"No, she'll meet us at the mall."

"Oh goody! I like to see Grandma. I miss her when I don't see her."

~~~

On Saturday morning, after breakfast, Addie's mother said, "Addie, we need to leave as soon as possible. Your grandmother will be waiting for us. Bring a sweatshirt. You might need it."

Addie sped like lightning to her room. She grabbed her favorite sweatshirt from her dresser and a book about a girl who dreamt of becoming a ballerina.

Within minutes, Addie and her mother got into their shiny black car. They called it the Flying Eagle. Addie's mother turned the key. The car's engine rumbled and they took off!

~~~

When Addie and her mother arrived at the mall, Addie spotted her grandmother standing in front of the main entrance. She was wearing a black top, slacks, and flat shoes with sequins. Her red hair was glistening in the sun.

"Grandma," Addie yelled, running up to her, "I hope you find a blouse you like for your birthday."

"I do too! I need one to go with a new suit I bought."

When the doors to the mall swung open, Addie's mother headed for her favorite fashion store. Addie's hair bounced in the air as she skipped ahead of her.

While Addie's mother and grandmother looked at blouses, Addie tossed her sweatshirt and book on a chair and scooped up a silky purple scarf and a purple knitted beanie. She draped the scarf around her shoulders, flipped the beanie on her head, and strutted around. "I'm a queen. I rule over this spot!" she said. Twirling around, she saw her reflection in a mirror. She turned her head to the right, then to the left and smiled. How pleased she was with what she saw! Afterwards, she turned a cartwheel. No one saw her.

Working her way up and down the aisles, Addie spun like a ballerina in a music box, turning then looking, turning then looking. Eventually, she slipped on her sweatshirt and sat down to read her book while her mother went to find a sales clerk.

After Addie had read her book for about ten minutes, her grandmother came over to her and said, "I found a blouse I like, but I've been thinking about you. What would you like for your birthday?"

Addie glanced up. "Grandma, my ninth birthday is four months away."

"Yes, I know, but what would you like?"

"I know what I want. I want to be a big sister. That's it!"

"My! That's a very special thing to want. Have you told your parents?"

"Uh-huh, about a zillion times, but I'm not giving up. Sophie, my doll, helps me make my wish every night. We send it to the brightest star. It's the luckiest one!"

"You do? I was an only child, too, but I was fine with it. I had paper dolls to play with. They kept me company. How the hours drifted away when I played with them!"

Addie felt her heart beat faster. Her grandmother had never mentioned paper dolls before. Her eyes widened. "What are paper dolls?"

"They're cardboard dolls. Many years

ago, they were very popular. We punched out a cardboard doll and the paper clothes that came with her."

"Did you have many paper dolls to play with, Grandma?"

"I had quite a few. My mother gave me one for each holiday. I received my first one on Valentine's Day."

Addie's curiosity grew. She wondered if her grandmother still had any of her paper dolls. "Did you save any of them?" she asked.

"I did! I saved some of the newer ones. I wonder if I saved enough of them to send you one during each holiday. Would you like that?"

"Oh, yes!" Addie said, jumping to her feet.

"I'll get busy and hunt for them," her grandmother said.

"Hooray!" Addie said. "I'll keep my fingers crossed." In the blink of an eye, she crossed her fingers, raised them high above her head, and held them there for a long, long while.

2

Move Faster "Shorty!"

On Monday morning, Addie arrived at school early. Mary Ellen snuck up behind her. "Boo!" she said. "Take a look at my brand-new sneakers." They were bright red and had drawings of chocolate chip cookies on them.

"They're spectacular!" Addie said. "Can you run faster in these sneakers than you did in your old ones?"

"I think so," said Mary Ellen. "I'll find out at P.E." They continued talking as they lined up for class.

Soon their teacher, Mr. Sloane, hurried out to the schoolyard. He greeted his students and led them into the classroom. He was stout and had short brown hair and hazel eyes. Once everyone was seated, he passed out a math quiz.

Later that morning, once they had completed their quiz and other assignments, Mr. Sloane took his third-grade students out to the schoolyard for their physical education class. Mr. Del Toro, the P.E. teacher, was outside waiting for them, standing straight and tall in his baseball cap. "Are you ready to play kickball?" he yelled.

"Yes!" they all shouted.

A boy and a girl were chosen to be team captains. While they chose their teams, Mr. Del Toro took a thick piece of chalk and drew four bases. Afterwards each captain chose a pitcher, a catcher, and three team members to guard each base.

Mr. Del Toro flipped a coin to determine which team would get to kick the ball first.

One student after another kicked the ball. When it was Mary Ellen's turn, she gave it a good hard kick and zoomed all the way to third base.

Soon it was Addie's turn. She kicked it and took off running toward first base when Oliver, a student in her class, called out, "Move your legs faster, Shorty!"

Shorty? Addie turned around and glared at Oliver.

Immediately, the first baseman tagged Addie out.

"See! I told you to run faster," Oliver shouted.

Mr. Del Toro walked over to Oliver. He told him to settle down and to move to the end of the line.

Addie plopped down on the bench and crossed her arms. *That Oliver! He should talk, with his freckled face and spiked hair,* she thought. *I wish he'd go back to his old school!* He had been teasing Addie since the day he joined their class three weeks ago. He had recently moved from Idaho to Arizona and had started school much later than everyone else.

~~~

As soon as Addie got home from school, she looked for her father. She saw him sitting on the sofa in the living room. He was stroking his mustache while reading the newspaper. She sat down next to him. "Dad, why do some kids like to bother other kids?" she asked.

Her father stopped reading the newspaper and put it down. "What? Is someone bothering you?"

"Yes, a boy named Oliver. He called me Shorty."

"He did? I wonder why he'd say that. Hmm, I'll be right back!" He left to search for his tape measure. When he returned, he stood Addie up against a wall, right beside their old grandfather clock. He measured her height. "I wouldn't pay any attention to him. You're just the right height for your age."

"Thanks, Dad. No one's ever called me Shorty before. I can't figure out why Oliver would say that."

"You never know, Missy, what boys are thinking," her father said, calling her by her nickname. "Maybe he likes you and is trying to get your attention."

"What? Likes me? Yuck! That's the last thing I want!"

"Well, when I was in school, I teased girls I liked," her father explained.

"What? You were like Oliver?" Addie shook her head. "I don't understand why boys act like that."

"I know it's hard to understand right now, but someday you will."

Addie shook her head and went to her room. She dragged out her backpack and rummaged for her homework. When Addie finished her homework, her mother walked into her room. "Addie, your grandmother just phoned. She wants us to stop by her office so she can give you a gift."

Addie's face brightened. "A gift? What kind of gift?"

"Your grandmother didn't say. I think she wants to surprise you."

"Surprise me? Whoopee! I wonder if she found one of her paper dolls?"

"We'll just have to wait and see." Addie locked her fingers together and drew them close to her heart. She couldn't wait to find out!

~~~

When Addie and her mother arrived at the shoe store where her grandmother worked, the door to Grandma Estelle's office was halfway closed. "Someone's with her," Addie's mother whispered. "She's busy. Why don't we look at some shoes?" Addie's mother headed toward the high-heeled shoes. A

14

store clerk named Camilla walked over to her.

Addie picked up a pink boot from the display rack. She quickly removed her right shoe and slipped it on. "Ta-da!" she said, joyfully extending her arms. Within minutes, she spotted a woman leaving her grandmother's office. She shook the boot off and scooped up her shoe. She scampered into the office. "Hi, Grandma! I could hardly wait to see you," she said. Then she sat down to put her shoe back on.

Her grandmother smiled. "Addie, I'm so glad you came. Guess what? I have something for you!" Addie's grandmother opened her desk drawer and pulled out an orange envelope.

"Did you find a paper doll?"

"I sure did. I was determined to find one for you."

"Thank you, Grandma." Addie took the envelope. "I was hoping you'd find one."

"You are so welcome. Paper dolls are such great company, and I can't tell you how happy I am that you've shown an interest in them. Your mother never did."

"I'm sure if I had a little sister, she'd want to play with them too."

Addie clutched the envelope and pulled out a paper doll with light brown hair and green eyes. She also pulled out the doll's outfits. One of her outfits was a cheerleading outfit with white sneakers, two red and white pompoms, and a red megaphone. The other outfit was a short-sleeved white blouse, a pink poodle skirt, and a pair of black sandals with wide straps.

"Grandma, I like my doll's cheerleading outfit. Maybe someday I'll be a cheerleader just like her. 'Valor' is a word I learned at school today. It means 'bravery.' I'll name her Valery because cheerleaders are brave. They do lots of high jumping stunts."

"That's a perfect name for her. She can keep you company and help you to be courageous," her grandmother said.

Addie saw her mother coming with a shoe bag in her hand. "Did you buy a pair of shoes?" she asked.

"I sure did! I bought a pair of gray high-heeled shoes that hug my feet."

"Look at my paper doll and all of her outfits!"

"My! What a splendid gift!" her mother

said.

"Mom, I want Mary Ellen and Tiana to see my paper doll. Can they come over this Saturday if their parents say they can?"

"Of course!" her mother replied, "Go ahead and invite them."

Addie glowed. She couldn't keep still. Her feet began to dance and twirl her around the room!

3

You Look Hilariously Ridiculous!

On Saturday afternoon, Addie kept her eyes glued to the wall clock in the living room. Mary Ellen and Tiana had promised they would arrive at one o'clock.

Ding-dong! At exactly one o'clock, the doorbell rang. Tiana and Mary Ellen were standing at the door.

Before they could even hang up their jackets, Addie said, "Come to my room. I want to show you something." She had dressed Valery in her cheerleading outfit and held her up so Mary Ellen and Tiana could see her. "Look! My grandmother gave me this paper doll! She played with her when she was my age."

Mary Ellen and Tiana looked at her

19

light brown hair, green eyes, and cheerleading outfit, their eyes practically jumped right out of their sockets. "She's the coolest thing I've ever seen!" said Tiana.

"Double wow!" said Mary Ellen. "I've never seen a paper doll before! She's fabulous!"

Mary Ellen and Tiana took turns dressing Valery and fussing over her. While they were playing with her, Addie told them how much she wanted to be a big sister.

"I've always thought you were lucky not to have a brother or a sister," said Mary Ellen. "Sometimes they get into your things and then you can't find them."

"That's true," said Tiana. "My brother likes to hide my things. He thinks it's funny. He calls it playing hide and seek." She groaned.

"Really, I've never thought about that,"

Addie said. Their stories weren't enough to make her change her mind. After they had played with Valery, Addie laid out sketchpads, crayons, markers, pencils, and erasers so they could color and draw. They tossed around truckloads of ideas of what to draw, but they couldn't decide. "I know!" Addie said. "Why don't we draw pictures of what we want to be when we grow up?"

"That's a great idea," said Mary Ellen. "I want to be a preschool teacher."

"I want to be a veterinarian," said Tiana. "I love animals."

"I want to be an actress," said Addie. "I like to pretend I'm somebody else. To me, that's exciting!"

After they'd drawn their pictures and displayed them all around Addie's room, Tiana said, "Why don't we play dress up?"

With great gusto, Addie swung open

her closet doors, where she kept some clothes her mother had given her to play with. She also pulled out her bureau drawers. "Choose any clothes you like!" she said.

"Can we wear anything we want?" asked Tiana.

"Sure!" Addie said. "Let's have fun! I want to look ridiculous."

"Great!" Mary Ellen exclaimed. "Show us how ridiculous you can look."

Addie slipped on a long black skirt with a wide band that dragged on the floor and a yellow blouse with short sleeves and a drawstring neck that was way too big. She stepped into a pair of high-heeled shoes that flip-flopped on her feet when she walked. She brought out a box of costume jewelry her grandmother had given her and flung red, gold, green, and silver beads around her neck. She slipped a multi-colored link bracelet around her right wrist and clipped on a pair of oval turquoise earrings. To top it all off, she clipped a huge pink bow in her hair.

When Addie had finished dressing, Mary Ellen and Tiana exploded with laughter. They flopped down on her bed holding their sides, doubled over laughing.

"You look hilariously ridiculous!" said Tiana as she continued to laugh.

The rest of the afternoon, Addie, Mary Ellen, and Tiana dressed up trying to look as ridiculous as they could. They jogged back and forth looking at their outfits in the mirror. They'd say to each other, in an exaggerated way, "You look marvelous! Simply marvelous!"

Tiana and Mary Ellen took turns scooping up a pen and a small tablet. They'd inch close to Addie and say, "May I have your autograph?" Addie giggled and posed like a swan. She pretended she was a famous person and signed her name in big fancy letters.

Before Mary Ellen went home, she said, "I've had a funlicious time, Addie! We have to do this again."

"We sure do!" Tiana said. "I wish I could

come back tomorrow."

~~~

Later that evening, after Addie had taken Sophie in her arms and made her wish, she crawled into bed and thought about Mary Ellen and Tiana. She imagined what it would be like if they were her sisters instead of her friends.

Then as she dozed off to sleep, she whispered, "I'm a feather floating up to the land of dreams."

4

The Turkey Twins

A few days before Thanksgiving, Addie was in her room busily coloring and cutting out small paper turkeys she had made. Her father called out to her, "Addie, Grandma's here!"

Addie scooped up one of her turkeys and ran to greet her grandmother. "Here, Grandma, I made this turkey for you."

"My! What a wonderful turkey! He looks like he's smiling. I'll put him on my refrigerator so I can see him every day."

"I'm glad you like him," Addie said.

"I have something for you too."

"You do? What did you bring me?"

"I found two more paper dolls." She reached into her large handbag, pulled out two yellow envelopes, and handed them to Addie.

27

Addie shook out two paper dolls from the first envelope. They had blonde hair and blue eyes. "They looked exactly alike. They're twins!" Addie exclaimed. "They'll always have each other. I will name them Kari and Kara." She shook out their wardrobe from the second envelope. She saw jeans, skirts, blouses, shoes, hats, sweaters, jackets, and coats.

Addie was so excited. She threw her arms around her grandmother, "Thank you, thank you, thank you, Grandma! I am so glad you saved your paper dolls for me to play with. I love you, Grandma."

"I'm grateful too, for so many things," Grandma said. "Gratitude lives in my heart. I have so many happy memories."

Addie thought about gratitude living in a person's heart. She closed her eyes and felt gratitude in her heart too.

Later, after her grandmother left, Addie rushed to her room to make her a thank-you card. She wanted to thank her grandmother for Kari and Kara. First, she drew pumpkins all around the edges of the card. After that, on the left side, she drew a round basket filled with oranges and apples. Last of all, on the right side, she drew a picture of herself with a toothy smile and wrote the words THANK YOU.

When Addie had finished making her card, she took it to her mother and asked her to mail it for her. Then she went to her room. She picked Sophie up and looked out her window at the night sky. "Sophie," she said, "it's time to make our wish. Let's close our eyes real tight. No peeking! Don't let any light in. Now let's make our wish." *Swoosh!*

How long do I have to wait? Addie thought. *When will my wish come true?*

29

~~~

The next morning, when Addie arrived at school, she thought about making two turkeys during art class because she wanted them to be twins like Kari and Kara. She thought about making five feathers for each turkey and putting three colors on each feather. She whispered aloud, "My turkeys will be rainbow turkeys." All morning, as Addie completed her class work, she imagined how her turkeys would look.

Finally, in the afternoon, Addie and her classmates buzzed around their classroom, as they got ready for their art class. On a piece of poster board, they traced a turkey's head, body, and feathers. Like musical notes strung together, they worked in groups of four. They shared glue, scissors, markers, and watercolor paints.

Addie said to her group, "I'm going to

make two turkeys. I want them to be twins and look exactly alike."

"Me too!" said Betsy, who always kept a pile of books on her desk.

Addie worked diligently, adding three colors on each of her feathers, but after a while, she looked puzzled. She glanced around for a missing feather. "Has anyone seen one of my feathers? I cut out ten, but now I have nine." She checked to see if it had fallen on the floor. "That's strange! It was right here! How did it disappear? Does anyone have an extra one?"

"I saw Oliver nab your feather when he passed by your desk a couple of minutes ago," said Mani, a boy with a short ponytail on the top of his shaved head.

"So did I," said Stuart, who sat next to him. "I saw him grab other ones too."

Addie put her hands on her hips. "Not

Oliver again!" she groaned. She sped over to his desk.

When Oliver saw Addie heading his way, he reached for the pile of feathers on his desk and sat on them. Addie caught sight of what he had done and turned around and marched right over to Mr. Sloane. She mentioned she was missing a feather. She also mentioned that Oliver had been seen nabbing it and other ones too.

Mr. Sloane asked if anyone else was missing a feather. Five hands shot into the air. "I am! I am!" echoed across the room.

Then he went over to Oliver's desk to talk to him about the missing feathers.

Oliver denied he had them.

"That's not true," Addie said. "He's sitting on them."

Oliver got up. "Here!" he said, hastily scooping up the feathers. "I don't want them. I was just kidding."

"You'll need to see me after school," Mr. Sloane said. He continued, "Those of you missing feathers, come and get them."

Addie's feather was messed up. She couldn't use it because it was wrinkled and torn. A tear ran down her cheek. *Remember to be brave,* she told herself.

Once the commotion over the missing feathers quieted down, Mary Ellen sneaked over to see Addie. "I'm sorry Oliver messed up your feather."

"He ruined it. Now my turkeys can't be twins."

"They're still super cool," said Mary Ellen. "They have gobs of colors on them."

"My turkeys are rainbow turkeys, but one's missing a feather," Addie complained.

"It's still neat though," said Mary Ellen.

At the end of the day, Addie slipped

her turkeys into a folder and put them in her backpack.

~~~

Once the dismissal bell had rung, Addie walked outside to look for her mother. She saw their car was parked on the right side area of the schoolyard. When Addie slid into their car, her mother said, "Addie, your grandmother called this morning to let you know she received her thank-you card and loved it." Then her mother asked, "How was your day at school?" They sat in the car as Addie went on and on about her ruined feather. She let her mother know how disappointed she was her turkeys couldn't be twins.

"I'm sorry you had such an upsetting day," her mother said. "Why don't you show me your turkeys?" Addie unzipped her backpack and showed them to her.

"They're brilliant," her mother said. "They're as colorful as a box of crayons."

"Yeah, but since one of my feathers is ruined, they don't look like twins. They look odd. They don't look the way I wanted them to look. They look different."

"They're still beautiful," her mother said. "You're very creative, and that's something to be thankful for."

Addie studied her turkeys once again. "I guess it's not so bad to be different," she said. "Besides, they'll always have each other, just like brothers and sisters always have each other."

~~~

Days later, while Addie played in her room with her turkeys, she gazed at the colors on their feathers and admired them. She told them they looked perfectly fine to her, and she no longer thought they were odd. "I think you're pretty," she said, "I didn't think you were before, but I do now." Then she picked them up and danced around the room.

5

Oliver's Recess Antics

Before too long, the month of November slipped away and Addie flipped her calendar to December. How she looked forward to having a holiday break! Each morning, before she left for school, she'd mark a day on her calendar. She was keeping track of how many days were left until Christmas. "There are twenty-one days left," she whispered. *I wonder if my wish will come true for Christmas.*

Once Addie had marked her calendar, she placed Sophie, Valery, Kari, and Kara on top of her dresser. "I'm Charisse, a famous ballerina. I'm a star!" she said. "People all over the world know about me. I'm graceful and swift like a gazelle, and now I'm going to show you my dance routine." Addie twirled around, lifted her arms up, and arched them. She swayed to the right and then to the left. She continued swaying, tilting, gliding, and sidestepping until she side-stepped out of her bedroom door and bumped into her father.

"Whoa, Missy!" her father said.

"Sorry!"

"Hey, Missy, aren't we supposed to be leaving for school now?"

~~~

At school, when her class went out for recess, Addie showed Mary Ellen and Tiana the dance routine she had been practicing earlier. They practiced learning it for a long while. Then Mary Ellen and Tiana decided they wanted to play ball. Addie wanted to sit on a bench for a few minutes.

While Addie sat on the bench, a ball rolled up and hit her foot. She saw Jamie, a fifth grader with braces on her teeth, motioning to her to send it back. Addie was all set to toss it back to Jamie when Oliver skidded in front of her. He knocked the ball out of her hands, caught it, and then held it away from her. "Stop being such a nuisance, Oliver! That's not your ball!" Addie said.

Oliver shrugged his shoulders. "So? Who cares?"

"I do! I care. Give it to me!"

The recess monitor, Mrs. Chiu, who wore a bucket hat with the brim pulled down, heard Addie and Oliver arguing and went over to them. She took the ball away from Oliver before benching them both. She instructed them to sit at opposite ends of the bench. After that, she took off to help a boy who had fallen and skinned his knee.

Addie made her way over to her side of the bench and plopped down. She stomped her foot. This was the first time she'd ever been benched. "Oliver!" she hollered. "I shouldn't have to sit on the bench! I didn't do anything wrong! Why didn't you give me the ball?"

Oliver ignored Addie. He stared straight ahead and watched a kickball game. He jumped up and down and cheered every time his team scored a point. All the while, he kept track of Mrs. Chiu. Addie continued to fume while she waited for Oliver to respond. It seemed to her like a hundred minutes had passed when Oliver hollered back. "It wasn't your ball! Why did you have to make such a fuss?"

What fuss? Addie wondered. *All I wanted was for Jamie to have her ball back.* She chose to remain mum. Oliver stretched his body to the left and slid over a little closer toward Addie. He repeated what he had said. Instantly, Mrs. Chiu gave him a signal to move back. He slid back to his place and looked over at Addie. He became squirrelly, sliding toward Addie ready to say something to her and sliding back whenever Mrs. Chiu turned around to check on him. Mary Ellen and Tiana had snuck over to talk to Addie, but Mrs. Chiu had circled the yard and quickly dismissed them. Then she walked away and headed for the opposite end of the yard. Immediately, Emilio kicked a ball over to Oliver, who kicked it back to him, sending it flying eight feet in the air.

Addie stayed silent. Her mouth felt dry and like someone had clamped it shut. She closed her eyes and imagined she was on a sailboat sailing across a clear blue lake. All of a sudden, she shrieked, and then jumped to her feet. Oliver had scooted across the bench and had tapped her on the shoulder.

She twirled toward the bench and looked into a smiling, freckled face. Oliver was about to utter a few words when Addie yelled at him and said, "Get away from me, Oliver! I hope Mrs. Chiu catches you and benches you at lunchtime."

Oliver said, "Okay! Forget it!" He hightailed it back to where he had been sitting and began to bite his fingernails. For the remainder of their recess period, they both sat as still as the pavement beneath their feet. When it was time to get off the bench, Oliver turned toward Addie and called out, "I wish you were like Melissa Stuart!"

"Melissa Stuart? Who is Melissa Stuart?" Addie mumbled aloud. At that moment, Mary Ellen and Tiana skipped over to her. She told them what Oliver had said.

"I've never heard of anyone by that name at this school," Mary Ellen said.

"Neither have I," said Tiana.

No one seemed to know anyone by the name of Melissa Stuart. So Addie began to think she was someone who lived in Oliver's memory.

6

Faith, Hope, and Charity

When Addie arrived home from school, she read for a while, but she couldn't stop thinking about what Oliver had said to her. She closed her book. Then she went looking for her mother. She found her in her home office, working on her laptop.

"Mom, today Oliver said he wished I was like Melissa Stuart. No one at school knew anyone by that name. Do you know who she is?"

Her mother glanced up from the screen. "Melissa...Melissa Stuart. No, I don't."

"What? I thought you'd know. Don't grownups know everything?"

Smiling, her mother said, "We're knowledgeable about many things, but we don't know everything. I wish I knew who she was and could help you. Oh, and I almost forgot." She pointed at a large envelope on the hall table. "Your grandmother came by earlier and left something for you."

Addie's face brightened. It had to be more paper dolls! She sashayed over to the hall table and picked up a brown envelope. She ripped it open and shook out three paper dolls. "Wow!" Addie called out. "Grandma left me three paper dolls this time! They don't look like triplets."

"How delightful!" her mother called

back.

Addie jiggled the envelope and a note fell out. She read it to herself. After she had read it, she zipped into her mother's office. She showed her mother the three paper dolls her grandmother had sent her. "Grandma wrote me a note. The note says she named these dolls Faith, Hope, and Charity. They look as if they're best friends. They remind me of Mary Ellen, Tiana, and me. We're best friends."

"What a splendid gift!" her mother said, and then she paused. "You know, Addie, I need to go to the post office. If you like, we can stop by the shoe store on the way home so you can thank your grandmother for the new dolls. Would you like that?"

"Oh, yes!" Addie said.

~~~

When Addie and her mother arrived at

the shoe store, a car pulled up right behind them. "Addie," her mother said, "your grandmother just pulled up behind us."

"She did?" Addie swung around to look for her grandmother.

"Let's wait here for a minute. I'll roll down the window."

Addie's grandmother hurried over to their car. "Grandma," Addie said, "we all got here at the same time."

"Yes, I'm glad I didn't miss you."

Addie's mother said, "Mom, I need to pick up some coffee Joe likes. It won't take me long."

"Go ahead, Cora. There's no need for you to rush."

"I'll be back in a few minutes, Addie," her mother said.

"Come on, Addie," her grandmother said. "Let's go inside and get comfortable."

When they stepped inside the shoe store, Addie waved to Camilla, who was busy helping a customer.

After they reached her grandmother's office and sat down, Addie said, "Grandma, my dolls, Faith, Hope, and Charity are terrific! Thank you! Thank you! Why did you choose those names?"

"I didn't choose them, my mother did," her grandmother replied. "She explained to me that faith would remind me to believe in my dreams. Hope would remind me not to give up on them, and charity would remind me to think of others."

"I like that," Addie said. She and her grandmother chatted some more about her paper dolls. Before too long, Addie talked to her grandmother about Oliver. She wanted her to know all about him. She mentioned how he had said he wished she were like Melissa

Stuart.

"Does her name sound familiar to you?" Addie asked.

"No, it doesn't. Why don't you ask Oliver who she is?"

"Who? Me?" Addie said, pointing to herself.

"Yes, from what you've told me, it sounds to me like Oliver might be trying to get your attention. Who knows, he might want to be your friend but just doesn't know how. Perhaps you can help him by being friendly to him." Addie felt more confused than ever. She didn't know what to think.

~~~

The next day, before the school bell rang, Addie showed Mary Ellen and Tiana her new paper dolls. She had them hidden in a small nylon bag. "Look at what my grandmother gave me. Their names are Faith,

Hope, and Charity," she said.

"Addie, you're so lucky," said Mary Ellen. "They're fantastic!"

"They are so cool," Tiana said. "I love their names. I have a cousin whose name is Hope."

"I love their names too," Addie replied. "My great-grandmother named them and I've been thinking about what she said. Hope will remind me not to give up on my wish to be a big sister. My doll Faith will remind me to believe that my wish will come true, and my doll Charity will remind me to be kind to others."

Then Addie told them how her grandmother wanted her to be friendly with Oliver, and how she wanted her to ask him about Melissa Stuart.

"Eww, Addie," Mary Ellen said. "How can you be friendly with Oliver? He isn't nice to you."

"I know," said Tiana. "He's not nice at all."

Addie sighed. "Yeah, it doesn't make any sense to me either." *I suppose*, she thought, *my doll Charity could help me to be friendly to him.*

7

Honey is Sweeter Than Vinegar

As the Christmas season began, Addie thought about being friendly to Oliver, but whenever she saw him at school she didn't feel courageous enough to stop and talk to him. She decided not to think about him so much and soon she began to look forward to Christmas and her winter break.

Before too long, Addie was on her school break and her grandmother had come over to see her. She brought her some new outfits for her paper dolls. She and Addie sorted through all of the outfits, put them in envelopes, and labeled them.

Addie's grandmother also brought her an early Christmas gift wrapped in red tissue paper. Addie gasped as she separated the tissue paper and saw a doll with large brown eyes and dark brown hair. She carefully examined her long white dress, sparkling silver shoes, and gold dangling earrings that looked like Christmas balls. "Wow, Grandma! She looks like an angel. Watch her fly!" She swished the doll back and forth. "See! An angel is flying around us. I'll name her Angel."

"Yes, I can see that," her grandmother responded.

While Addie fussed over Angel, she and her grandmother continued to talk, and soon they were having a conversation about Oliver. She told her grandmother that she hadn't tried to be friendly to him.

"Addie, I have an idea for you," her grandmother said. "How about making a New Year's resolution?"

"What's a New Year's resolution?" Addie said, looking puzzled.

"At the beginning of every new year, people make a promise to either improve in some way or try something new. You could try something new by being friendly to Oliver, and that could be your New Year's resolution."

Addie looked bewildered. She wasn't sure she liked that idea. *I wish the New Year would bring me a brother or sister,* she thought.

Her grandmother continued talking. "Why don't you think about it? Anyway, a teaspoon of honey is much sweeter than a teaspoon of vinegar, right?"

"What does that mean?" Addie asked.

"It means that kind words are sweet like honey, and unkind words are bitter like vinegar."

Addie listened to her grandmother and thought about what she had said.

~~~

Soon after a joyful Christmas holiday, it was time for Addie to return to school.

One day, during the third grade students' art lesson, Mr. Sloane put a paper mat and a glob of clay on each person's desk. "Today," he said, "your art lesson will be to create a zoo animal to display in the classroom. You can work with a partner, in a small group, or alone."

A girl named Clarita, who liked to wear one of her father's old shirts for art class, joined Addie, Mary Ellen, and Tiana. Clarita wanted to make a lion. Mary Ellen and Tiana decided they wanted to make an elephant, and Addie didn't make up her mind right away. At first, she thought she'd make a hippo or a zebra, but instead chose to make a giraffe.

While Addie worked on her giraffe, she finally decided she would take her grandmother's advice to be friendly to Oliver.

She thought, *It's my resolution.* She left her seat to request a little more clay. On her way back, she walked over to Oliver's desk. He was working on a hippo all by himself. She gathered up her courage and said, "I like your hippo. It's neat!"

Oliver quickly looked up. "What?" he asked.

Addie pointed at his hippo and said, "I like your hippo. I thought about making a hippo, but I made a giraffe instead."

Oliver stared at Addie. He didn't know what to say. He looked perplexed.

"Have you ever heard that honey is sweeter than vinegar?" she asked.

"Huh?" he said, his forehead wrinkling. "What does that mean?"

Addie's courage began to fade. "Oh, forget it!" she said. Immediately, she made a beeline back to her table.

Mary Ellen and Tiana stared at her with their mouths wide open. They couldn't believe she had gone over to talk to Oliver. They were flabbergasted!

A week later, Addie noticed Oliver wasn't bothering her anymore. *Honey is sweeter than vinegar,* she thought. Grandma was right.

Even Mary Ellen and Tiana were surprised when one day at recess, Addie said, "Guess what? Oliver hasn't bothered me since I was friendly and talked to him."

"I'm glad," said Mary Ellen. "Most of the time, he upsets you." Tiana nodded her head in agreement.

Addie was thrilled Oliver was acting better toward her. She felt like humming.

8

My Trampled Cupcakes!

Addie looked forward to Valentine's Day. She had decided she wanted to give out cupcakes at school instead of cards. She and her mother baked many cupcakes the day before Valentine's Day. Addie thought her cupcakes looked perfect! She had spent hours decorating them with pink buttercream frosting shaped into rose buds. She'd added chocolate sprinkles on top and a few red candy hearts.

She made one for her teacher and one for everyone in her class, including Oliver. Her parents had reminded her she had decided to give out cupcakes instead of cards so she had to give him one too.

Addie didn't mind giving one to Oliver since he had been leaving her alone. She thought it was because she had been friendly to him. She wished she had been friendly a lot sooner.

On Valentine's Day, before Addie left for school, she heard her father calling her name from the hallway. "Addie," he said, "a package was just delivered for you, but there's no return address."

How Addie's hands tingled when she held the small package! It was wrapped in white paper that had red hearts drawn all over it. Inside the package lay a paper doll with rosy cheeks and a big red card shaped into a heart.

Her grandmother had written a poem on it especially for her. Addie read the poem to her father:

> Today my heart's a boiling kettle
> Cooking up some Valentines
> I can see them bubbling over
> Hear them shouting all the time,
> Hi there, cutie Addie-um!
> How you make my heart hum!
> Say you'll be my valentine,
> Say you'll be it all the time!
> Love, Grandma

"Grandma gave me my first valentine of the day and wrote a poem especially for me!" Addie exclaimed.

"I'm not surprised," her father said. "You're always the first person your grandmother thinks about."

Addie looked at her doll's rosy cheeks. "I will name you Rosie," she said.

After Addie played with Rosie for a few minutes, she and her mother packed up the cupcakes to take to school.

Addie's father stepped into the kitchen and joined them. "I came to see if I could help," he said. After he saw the cupcakes all neatly packed up, he said, "Those cupcakes look too delicious to pass up." He snuck one behind his back while Addie chuckled.

"Now, Joe," her mother said, "you can just put that cupcake back. We'll have one later. I put a few aside for tonight's dessert."

Five minutes later, her parents loaded up the car with Addie's cupcakes and took her to school.

~~~

When they arrived at school, her parents carried Addie's cupcakes, paper plates, and napkins into her classroom and set them on a side table. Before they left, they told Addie she was their most precious valentine every day of the year.

As soon as Addie took her seat, an announcement blared over the loudspeaker. Mr. Sloane asked everyone to quiet down so they could hear it. The principal said, "Happy Valentine's Day! Your teachers will let you know when you can pass out cards and have your parties. Until then, stay focused on your lessons."

They decorated oversized paper bags during art class to hold their valentines and patiently waited. After what seemed like a thousand years, they heard their teacher say, "It's time to clear your desks."

"Yes! Yes! Yes!" yelled Montel from the back of the room, He had been lining up ten pencils side by side on his desk.

"Finally!" said Phil. He sprang to his feet and looked around.

Their desktops could be heard closing. Some banged. The noise in the room rose higher and higher as everyone rushed to put away their things.

"I'll call your names in groups," said Mr. Sloane. "So you'll know it's your turn to pass out your cards."

Addie couldn't wait for her name to be called. To Addie, her cupcakes were superb!

Mr. Sloane said, "Tristan, Addie, Marisa, and Oliver, please pass out your Valentine's Day cards." Everyone in Addie's group darted around the room as they dropped their cards into decorated bags. The Valentine's Day cards were being read and reread, counted and recounted.

Addie asked Mary Ellen and Tiana to help her pass out the small paper plates and napkins she had brought. While everyone waited for their cupcakes, they had fun telling each other stories and jokes. Their laughter rose to the ceiling and spilled into the hallway.

Once the paper plates and napkins had been passed out, Addie smiled and picked up a tray of cupcakes. Suddenly, someone sailed by and knocked into her. Cupcakes flew into the air and splattered on the floor. Everyone gasped.

It was Oliver.

Addie felt her temperature rise. Her body got hotter and hotter. "Oliver!" she bellowed. "Look what you've done! You've ruined my cupcakes! Valentine's Day is ruined!"

"Sorry! I'm sorry! I really am!" he said.

Four or five students quickly tried to help Addie pick up her cupcakes.

Oliver repeated again, "I'm really sorry." Then, as he tried to move away, he stepped on one of Addie's cupcakes. Everyone gasped again. He quickly lifted his left leg up and saw his shoe had buttercream frosting on it and red hearts clinging to it.

"Oliver P. Newton!" Mr. Sloane said firmly. "How many times have I told you not to run in the classroom? It's not a speedway. Take off your shoe and go to the office."

Addie couldn't look at Oliver. Tears welled up in her eyes. She had been friendly to him, and he was still ruining everything for her. "That Oliver!" Addie exclaimed. She looked at the pink buttercream rose buds she had spent hours making smashed against the classroom floor.

Mary Ellen and Tiana tried to console Addie, but she slunk down in her seat and wouldn't say anything.

~~~

Soon after the bell rang, Addie met her parents in the school parking area. On the way home, Addie's father asked, "How's our favorite valentine?" Addie went on and on about Valentine's Day. Her parents inquired if Oliver had gotten into trouble with their teacher.

"He sure did! He was sent to the office, and he wasn't happy about it."

"I'm sure he wasn't," her father said.

"No, he didn't like that, but he ruined my cupcakes, and he ruined Valentine's Day for me. Nothing can change that."

"Not being able to enjoy Valentine's Day and share your cupcakes with everyone must have been tough on you," her mother said. "I know how hard you worked decorating them. You did an excellent job, and you and I have happy memories of us baking them together. Happy memories last forever."

~~~

Later that night, Addie was alone in her

room, as usual, with Sophie, Angel, and her paper dolls. She thought about happy memories. How she longed to share them with a little brother or sister!

Addie took Sophie in her arms and looked out her bedroom window. "Sophie," she said, "it's time to make our wish. Let's close our eyes real tight. No peeking! Don't let any light in. Now let's make our wish." *Swoosh!* Then they stood still and waited while the wish floated away and hooked up with the brightest star.

Immediately afterward, Addie's parents walked into her room hoping to cheer her up. "Your birthday is coming up next month," her father said. "Your mother and I want to know if you'd like to invite everyone in your class to come to our house for your party, and Grandma too. Would you like that?"

"Yes, but do I have to invite Oliver?"

Addie's parents told her if she wanted to invite her class to her birthday party, she would have to invite Oliver. How Addie wished her parents hadn't said that! Yet, way down in the deepest part of her, she knew it was the right thing to do.

9

Happy Birthday, Addie!

On the day of her ninth birthday, Addie rolled out of bed and ran to look at herself in the mirror. Was she taller? Did she look older? The thought of turning nine wrapped itself around her like a warm blanket. That is, until her stomach ached when she thought about Oliver coming to her party. She hoped he wouldn't ruin every game they played.

Addie spent the whole morning waiting for their wall clock to strike eleven o'clock. She listened to its ticking, *tick-tock, tick-tock, tick-tock.*

At last! It was eleven o'clock. It was time for everyone to start arriving! Addie and her grandmother kept an eye on the door.

Within seconds, the doorbell rang.

"Someone's here!" Addie said excitedly. She couldn't stop smiling. Her feet tap-danced with happiness. She opened the door as Mary Ellen's parents drove away.

Waiting at the door were Mary Ellen, Tiana, Betsy, and Clarita. Each one of them was holding a brightly wrapped gift. They wished her a happy birthday and gave her a group hug. More guests arrived. Her grandmother led them into the living room, where her parents welcomed them. The doorbell rang again.

Addie swung the front door open. Oliver was standing there. She didn't say a thing. He walked in and mumbled, "Happy Birthday, Addie." He tossed his jacket on the seat of a chair and shoved a small gift box under it.

Addie's grandmother came up beside her and greeted Oliver. "Welcome! You must be Oliver," she said cheerfully. "Let's join everyone else in the living room."

"Is everyone here?" her father asked.

"Yes, Joe, everyone that planned to come has arrived," Addie's mother replied.

"Today we're going to play a few games," Addie's father said. "Some of them go way back to when I was your age. Follow me!"

They followed Addie's dad outside to the backyard. He asked them to pair up. Then he grabbed a balloon and placed it between their backs. "Now press your backs together and pop your balloon," he said. Everyone paired up except for Oliver. He said he would sit this game out.

"Come and play this game with me, Grandma," Addie said. "I want you to be my partner."

Addie's grandmother smiled and joined

her. "I'm ready!" she exclaimed.

"Now please listen," Addie's mother said. "The first pair to pop their balloon will win a prize." They all pushed and pushed.

"Push harder, Grandma," Addie said.

Krishan and Emilio were partnered together. "I wish I had a safety pin," Emilio said, jokingly.

Mary Ellen was paired with Tiana. They both pushed back as hard as they could. They wriggled their shoulders up and down and pushed harder. They pushed and pushed until they heard a popping sound. They were the first ones to pop their balloon.

Mary Ellen and Tiana jumped up and down. "We did it!" Mary Ellen said.

"Hooray for you!" Addie's mother said. She gave them each a necklace with a dangling dolphin. They admired them for a while and moved off to the side. They helped each other put them on.

"Oh, pooh!" Addie said. She had tried so hard to win. She looked around to see what Oliver was doing and noticed he was stomping on a balloon that had been left on the ground. Emilio, Krishan, and Stuart had gone over to talk to him. "Now Oliver's acting like his old self," Addie whispered under her breath.

Addie's father walked up to Oliver and said, "Please hand me that balloon." Oliver handed it to him. "Thank you," her dad said. "I'm ready to start the next game. Why don't you and your friends come and join us?" Oliver hesitated for a moment, but he walked over and joined the group.

Addie was standing next to Tiana and said, "I can't tell if Oliver wants to be here or not."

"It's hard to tell," Tiana said, "but he

does seem different."

Addie's father gave each person in the group a spoon and a hard-boiled egg. "When you're ready," he said, "you can set the egg on the spoon. Don't forget to keep one hand behind your back. I've drawn a finish line." He pointed to it. "The first one to reach that line without dropping an egg will win a prize. We have a prize table set up with a few movies. You can pick the one you like."

"Are you ready?" Addie's mother asked.

"Yes!" they all shouted.

"One, two, three, go!" Addie's mother said.

Everyone moved forward. Eggs started spiraling, hitting the ground. Some cracked. Oliver stopped several times to steady himself. His plan worked. He was the first one to reach the finish line.

"Good for you!" Addie's mother said. "Come over here to the prize table and pick a movie."

Oliver high-fived Emilio, who had gone over to congratulate him, and jumped in the air. Together they walked over to the prize table so Oliver could choose a movie. He chose one about a white stallion.

Addie's father gave Oliver a thumbs up! Oliver grinned. "I did it!" he said.

After they'd finished their game, Addie opened her gifts. Tiana and Mary Ellen gave her paper dolls with punch-out clothes. She also received art supplies, a few T-shirts, a magic trick kit, and two word games. Addie beamed as she opened each gift. After she had thanked everyone for their gifts, Addie's mother said, "Let's have lunch! You must be hungry by now."

Addie's classmates sat around tables

her parents had set up on their patio. They were decorated with paper plates and napkins that had HAPPY BIRTHDAY written on them and huge pink, yellow, and purple balloons. There was also a party horn at each place. They ate pizza and drank lemonade. Addie couldn't wait to blow out the candles on her cake. Her grandmother had made her favorite chocolate cake with white frosting and strawberry filling in the middle. Addie couldn't look at it without her mouth watering! How delectable it looked!

Everyone gathered around Addie as her father lit the candles and her mother started the birthday song. When everyone had finished singing, they clapped for her and blew their party horns. Addie sat up straight and leaned forward to blow out her candles and make a wish. She was focused on her mouthwatering birthday cake and glowing birthday candles and hadn't noticed that Oliver was standing next to her. He wanted to get a better look at her cake. Addie knew exactly what her wish would be, and she was expecting it to come true. *I'm ready to send my wish to all the stars this time*, she thought. Addie closed her eyes, took in a deep breath, and blew hard.

When she opened her eyes, she saw that two of her candles were still lit. She took a deep breath once again, but before she could blow the two candles out, Oliver leaned forward and blew them out.

Everyone gasped and stared at Oliver.

"I can't believe you did that," said Mary

Ellen. "You just blew out Addie's birthday candles."

Oliver apologized. "I'm sorry," he said. "I was just trying to help her."

Everyone started complaining about what Oliver had done.

"Now, now," Addie's mother said, "these things happen."

Addie wasn't listening to Oliver or her mother at all. Oliver had just ruined her birthday wish. Her chest was pounding.

Oliver apologized and said, "I was just

trying to help you. I'm really sorry." He looked as red as a raspberry.

Addie didn't want to hear anything Oliver said. He had ruined her wish. She stood up and yelled, "Oliver, you're always ruining everything!" Without hesitation, she turned and hot footed it into the house.

~~~

When Addie got to her room, she grabbed Sophie and held her tight. Her mother followed. "Addie," she said, "everything will be okay. Come back and join us. Your father is ready to cut your cake. Everyone's waiting to have a piece."

"I can't, Mom! Why did you and Dad say I had to invite Oliver? He spoils everything. Look at what he's done!"

At that moment, Grandma walked into Addie's room. "I'll stay with her, Cora. Joe needs your help right now." She sat on the bed next to Addie. "Now Addie, why don't you tell me what's on your mind?"

Addie leaned against her grandmother, still holding Sophie. "Grandma, Oliver always ruins things for me."

"I know he does, but what just happened was different. He wanted to be helpful. He has apologized. Right this minute, he's slumped in a chair looking miserable."

"Why does he ruin everything for me, Grandma?" Addie went on about all of the other times Oliver messed things up for her.

Addie's grandmother listened and put her arm around her. "We need Kari and Kara. Where are they?" Addie got up from her bed and brought them to her grandmother. "Thinking about all the good things you have in your life will help you feel better. Why don't you name a few things you are thankful for?"

Addie began by saying she was thankful

for her parents, Mary Ellen, Tiana, and her paper dolls. She went on naming one thing after another. "I'm thankful for you, too, Grandma," she said.

"I'd say we're both very grateful to have each other. Now why don't we get back to your party? Your guests are waiting for you. Let's go have a slice of cake!"

"Okay, Grandma," Addie said as she slipped off her bed and took her grandmother's hand.

10

I Made It For You

Back at the party, everyone cheered when they saw Addie, and there was a big slice of cake waiting for her and her grandmother. Addie put a piece of cake in her mouth and smacked her lips. "Yum, Grandma," she said, grinning from ear to ear. "This cake is so, so delicious. I'm thankful for every bite I'm taking."

When they had finished eating Addie's scrumptious cake, her father said, "Now everyone follow me into the living room. We've hidden small notebooks, pencil sharpeners, erasers, stickers, pencils, and pens. You can keep whatever you find. Have fun looking for them!"

Addie's mother gave every guest a yellow paper bag as they went into the house.

"You're going to need this," she said.

Addie and her classmates snooped between sofa cushions, under chairs, and in cabinets. They ran around collecting every hidden gift they could find.

Oliver stayed away from the group. Addie's parents, Emilio, Krishan, Phil, Montel, and others tried to coax him to join in, but Oliver just shook his head.

After everybody had collected as many things as they could find, it was time to go home. Their parents were arriving and waiting to pick them up. Addie thanked each one of her classmates for coming to her party. Mary Ellen and Tiana hugged Addie as they walked out the door. Oliver quietly waited in the living room with Addie's parents and grandmother. His parents hadn't arrived yet.

When Oliver saw Addie had finished saying good-bye to everyone, he darted over to the chair where he had put his jacket. He scooped up the gift box he had shoved underneath it. He handed it to her. "Here, open this!" he said.

Addie's mother looked at Addie's father and at Grandma and whispered, "Why don't we leave them alone for a few minutes?"

Addie stared at the gift box in her hands. She undid the ribbon and opened the box. "Wow!" she said. Then she pulled out a card and a paper airplane.

"I made it for you," Oliver said, proudly.

"You made this!" Addie asked in disbelief. "No one has ever given me a paper airplane before."

"Read the message on the card."

Addie opened the card and read it. Across the top of the card were hand-drawn cupcakes and airplanes. "Dear Addie, I'm sorry I ruined your cupcakes and spoiled

Valentine's Day for you. I don't know how to make cupcakes, so I made you an airplane instead."

"I like your note, and I like this airplane," she said. It was a folded paper airplane with black and green designs on the top and bottom. It had a pointed nose and droopy wings. "Thank you, Oliver. I've never seen an airplane that looks like this one before."

"Your dad can help you fly it. Anyway, I'm sorry about what I did today. I ruined your birthday wish. I know I have a lot of other things to be sorry for too."

Addie wasn't use to Oliver acting nice. "Did your parents tell you to say that?" she asked.

"No," Oliver said.

"Are you sure?" Addie asked, looking straight at him.

Oliver smiled. "I'm sure."

Addie thought this might be a good time to ask Oliver about Melissa Stuart. "Who is Melissa Stuart?" she asked.

Oliver shuffled his feet. "She's a girl I knew at my other school. You remind me of her. We were friends, and I was friends with her brothers and sisters. I miss her. We teased each other and gave each other a hard time, but she'd always laugh. I guess I thought you were like her, but you aren't exactly alike."

"Nope," Addie replied, looking right at Oliver. "My name's different, and I'm different." Oliver chuckled. Addie thought he wasn't so bad after all. "Did you ever call Melissa, 'Shorty?'" she asked.

"No, I never did."

Addie told Oliver she didn't like being called Shorty. He promised he wouldn't call her Shorty anymore, and Addie knew she wouldn't be calling him "That Oliver!"

After Oliver left, Addie showed her parents and her grandmother the airplane he had made for her.

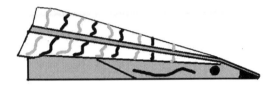

"What a fine gift!" her father said. "I suppose this means Oliver won't be giving you a bad time anymore."

"It's a splendid gift," her mother said. "You have a new friend."

"How wonderful!" her grandmother said. "I knew you could both work things out. Now I have something for you." She handed Addie a large yellow box wrapped with a huge polka dot bow.

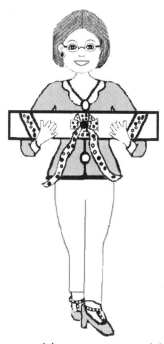

Addie quickly unwrapped her gift. She pulled out the most beautiful doll she had ever seen. It had rosy cheeks, long black hair, and blue eyes. She wore a silky yellow gown with crocheted daises on it and yellow ballerina slippers.

"This doll was as important to me as Sophie is to you," her grandmother said.

Addie gave her grandmother a bear

hug. "I hope I don't drop her."

Hanging across the doll's silky yellow dress was a white ribbon that read, "Happy Birthday, Addie," in pink scrolling letters.

Addie studied her doll for a moment. "You remind me of the daisies growing in our garden," she said. "I'm going to call you Daisy. You're my gorgeous Daisy and my special birthday gift. Thank you a hundred million times, Grandma. I will keep her forever. Thank you, Mom and Dad, a hundred million times, too, for my birthday party and for making me invite Oliver. We're friends now."

~~~

Later that evening, Addie thought about her friends, parents, grandmother, classmates, and Oliver. Everyone and everything meant more to her than mountains of gold. She sat on her bed with Sophie, Valery, Kari, Kara, Faith, Hope, Charity,

Angel, Rosie, and her new paper dolls gathered around her. She introduced them to Daisy.

After Addie had introduced Daisy to all of her dolls, her parents walked into her room. "Addie, we have an extra-special birthday present for you," her father said.

"I thought my birthday party was my present," Addie said. "That's what you told me."

"Yes," her mother said, "but what have you always wanted?"

Addie smiled and moved Sophie closer to her. "I've always wanted to be a big sister. I've wanted that more than I've wanted anything else in the whole world!"

"Well, guess what, Addie?" her mother said. "We have some good news. Soon your wish will come true! You'll have to wait a bit, but the day will come when you'll be a big sister."

Addie beamed. She jumped up, threw her arms around her parents, and hugged them. "See!" she said, looking up at them. "Wishes can come true! Today is the happiest day of my life!"

A Note to My Readers

Hello my dear readers,

Remember you, too, like Addie, can send your wish to the brightest star, if you use your imagination the same way she did. Say what you want, picture it, and send it up into the night sky. Perhaps, it too can hook up to a bright star. If not, it's okay. Swoosh! Send it off anyway!

Who knows? Maybe your wish, like Addie's, will come true!

Sincerely,
Gloria St. Joy

About the Author

After a lifetime of teaching young children, Gloria St. Joy still had more lessons to give. She began writing to help express them in the most favorable light. Her joy of teaching and her creative side is evident though the adventures of Addie in "Addie's One Wish to The Brightest Star."

A Special Thanks To

Cynthea Liu,
Maureen McInerney,
Laura Underhile,
Marie Sagues,
Annette Sheaffer,
Barbara Sullivan,
Angela Fabbri.
And in honor of Lucille Shea.

Made in the USA
San Bernardino, CA
22 April 2017